This book belongs to

....

Copyright © Tiny Owl Publishing 2021
Text and illustrations © Kate Milner 2021

Kate Milner has asserted her right under the Copyright, Designs and
Patents Act 1988 to be identified as Author and Illustrator of this work.

First published in the UK and US in 2021 by Tiny Owl Publishing, London.

For teacher resources and more information, visit
www.tinyowl.co.uk

#SorryMrsCake

A catalogue record for this book is available from the British Library.

A CIP record for this book is available from the Library of Congress.

UK ISBN 978-1-910328-73-6

US ISBN 978-1-910328-78-1

Printed in China

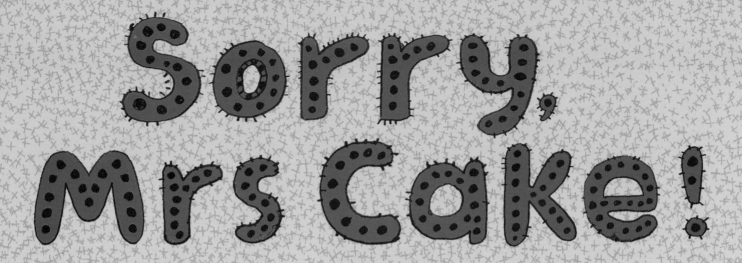

Sorry, Mrs Cake!

Kate Milner

TINY OWL

It's really noisy.
Do you think Mrs Cake will mind, Cat?
She's usually so quiet.
Don't ask me. I'm a cat.

I don't think they're listening, Mrs Cake.

Let's try the mums.

Maybe not.

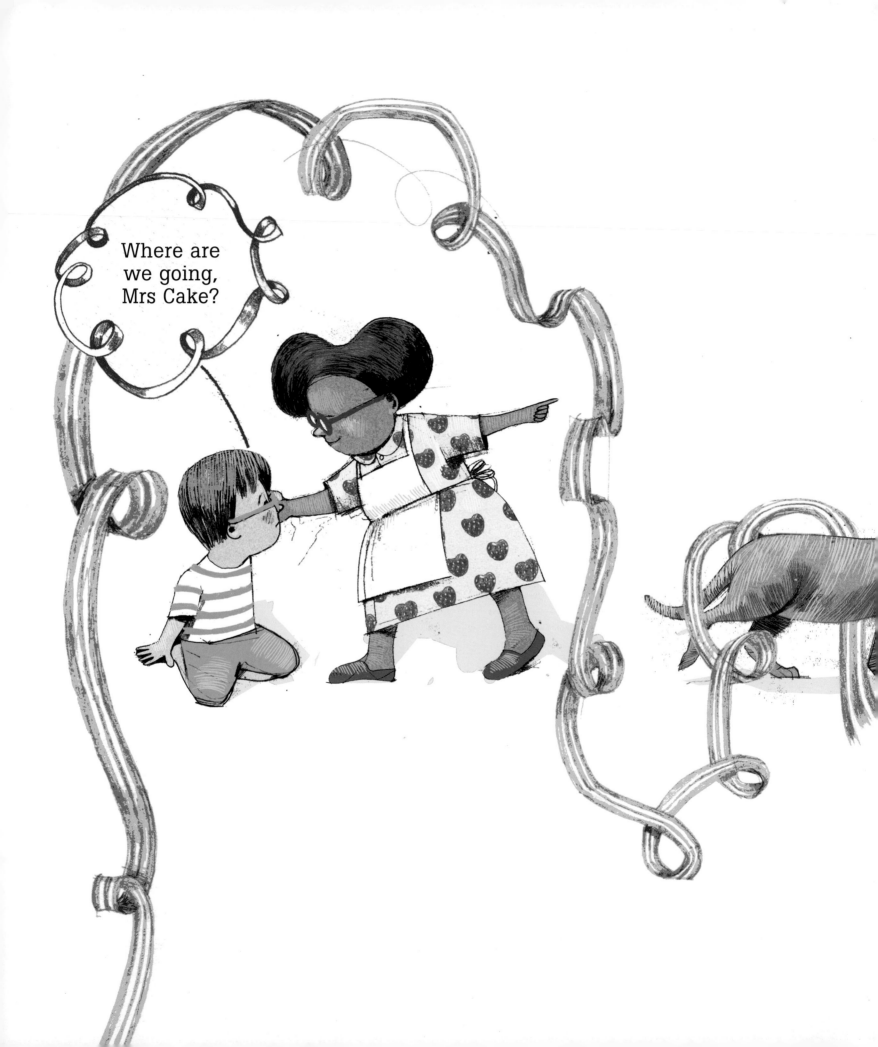

Wow!
Look at the feast you
have made, Mrs Cake.

And no one
knows about it
because they
didn't listen to us.

Guess what
my idea is...

You are
all very
welcome.